Created by Impact

A Young Enterprise company

Jelly and Friends

Go to School

Jelly woke up and jumped out of bed,
"I'm super excited for school", he said.

He wrote his name on his
little name tag,
and put his things in his
little book bag.

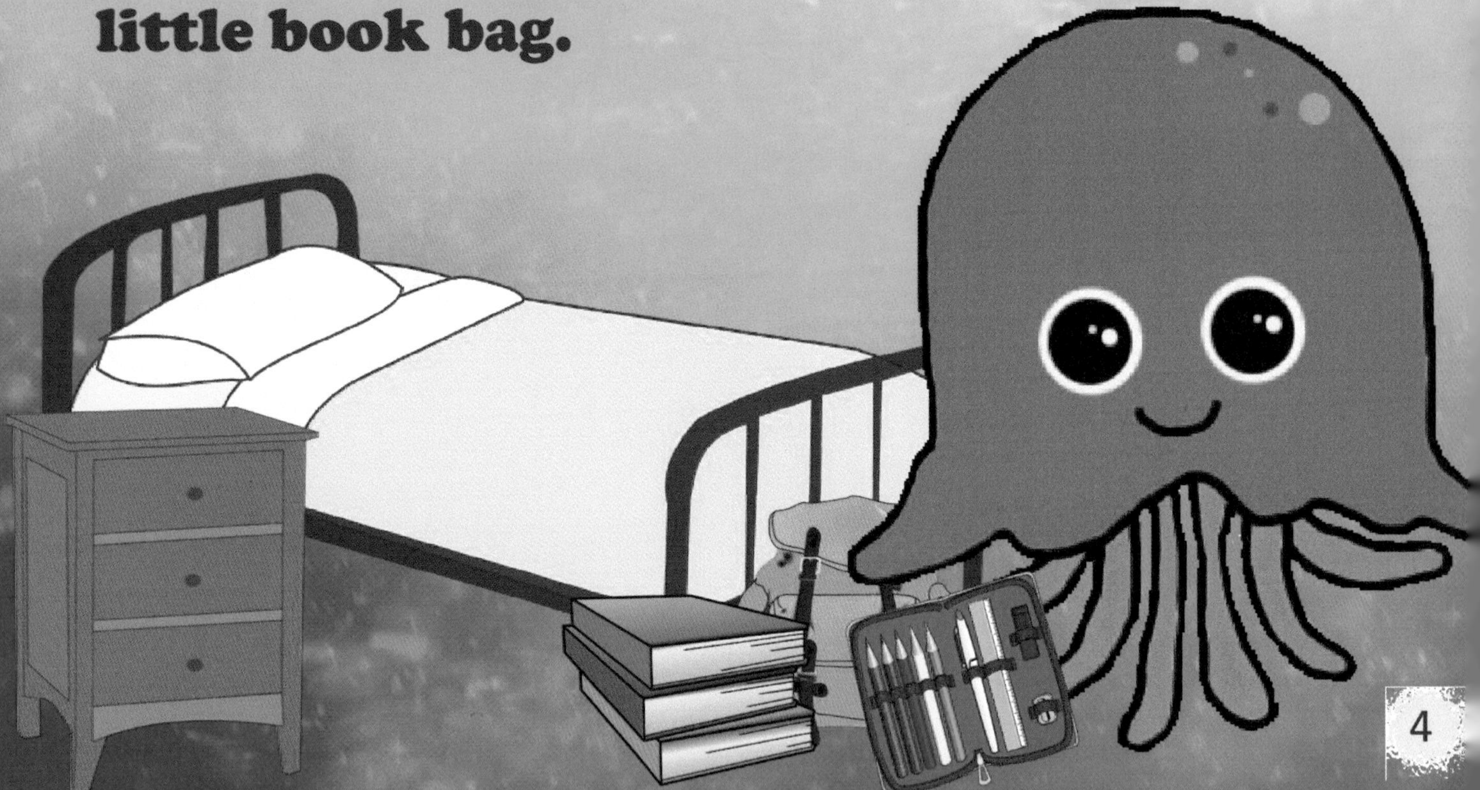

Can you help Jelly find his breakfast?

He cleaned his teeth with his brush,
and ran downstairs in a rush.

"Hello mummy I'm ready for school,
take a photo I look really cool!"

Choose Jelly's best school photo.

“We can’t be late on your first day!
Your school is in the barnacle bay,
It’s not really that far
away.”
Jelly needs to find his way.

Can you help Jelly?

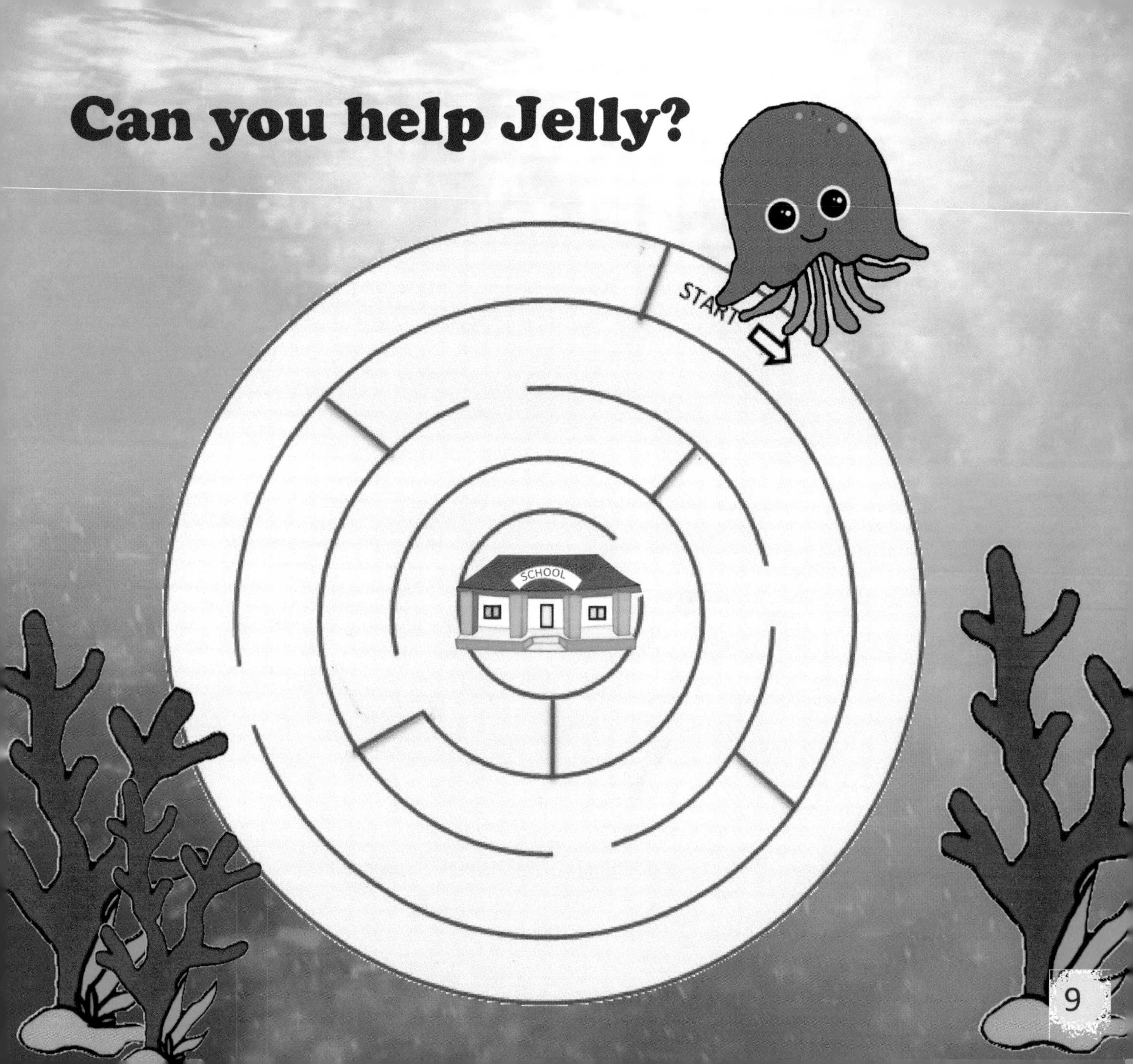

"We can cross now" his mum said. "The traffic lights have all turned red".

Look left and right before you go, the traffic isn't always slow.

Can you tell Jelly when to cross?

Jelly finally arrived at school,
and looked around to find a stool.
Jelly sat down on his seat,
excited about the friends he'd meet.

Can you find the empty stool for Jelly?

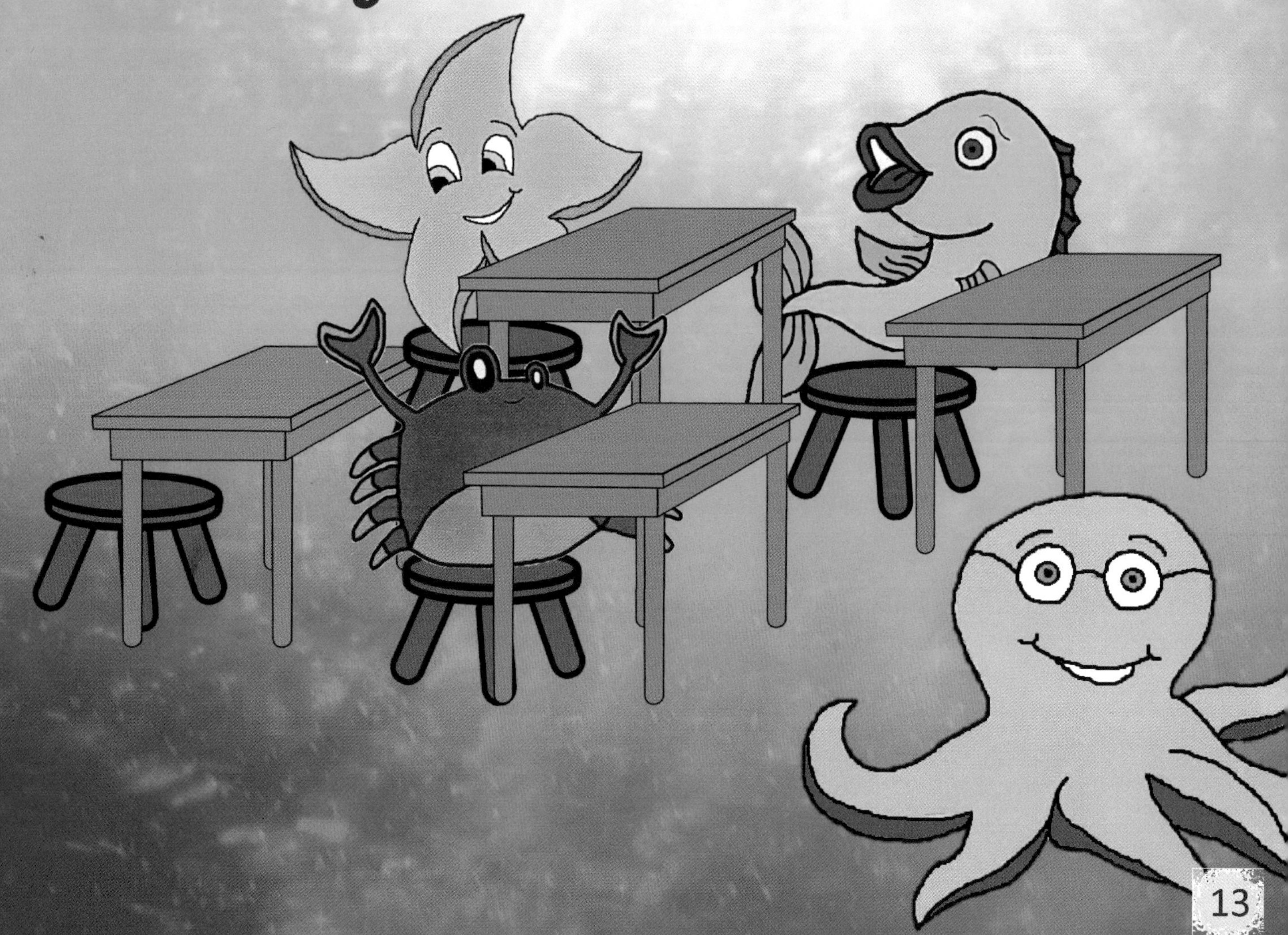

Mr Oscar stood at the front and said-

"Don't worry kids you have nothing to dread! School is fun and making friends is easy, I know I sound really cheesy!"

"Turn to the left and tell them your name,
Ask if they want to play a game.
Now off you go kids it's time for break!
How many friends can you make?"

Jelly and friends went out at break looking for more friends to make. He saw a starfish looking glum, so Jelly said "Hey I'll be your chum"

They played hide and seek all day long,
until Sally the Starfish realised she'd been wrong

"At first I was nervous about my first day at school.
Now I realise school does rule!"

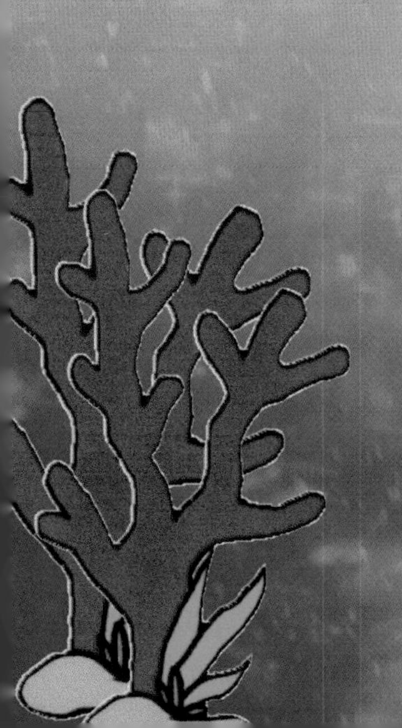

**Well done Jelly for making a friend!
Sadly the school day has come to an end.
Your parents are waiting at the gate.
See you tomorrow – don't be late!**

What time does school finish?

Jelly! Jelly! How was your day?"
"It was great mum, I learnt how to cross the road today!"
"Well done, I told you it's not as scary as it seems.
Now goodnight Jelly, sweet dreams!"

zZZ

Written, drawn and created by:

Hannah Fincham
Olivia James
Avneet Khaira
Nina Malmgren
Ria Patel
Shaana Sangar
Amber Thompson
Hannah Webb

ISBN-10: 1508556490
ISBN-13: 978-1508556497

10347446R00015

Printed in Great Britain
by Amazon.co.uk, Ltd.,
Marston Gate.